THE PATCHWORK PICNIC

The Patchwork Picnic
Hardie Grant Egmont
Ground Floor, Building 1, 658 Church Street
Richmond, Victoria 3121, Australia
www.hardiegrantegmont.com.au

A CiP record for this title is available from the
National Library of Australia.

Design by Stephanie Spartels
Typeset by Ektavo

1 3 5 7 9 10 8 6 4 2

Printed by McPherson's Printing Group, Maryborough, Victoria

The paper this book is printed on is certified against the
Forest Stewardship Council® Standards. FSC® promotes
environmentally responsible, socially beneficial and
economically viable management of the world's forests.

Lola's TOY BOX

THE PATCHWORK PICNIC

DANNY PARKER
illustrated by Guy Shield

hardie grant EGMONT

CHAPTER ONE

'Lola! Nick! Come downstairs,' called Mum. 'I'm having a clear out.'

Lola raced downstairs after her brother. Mum was standing at the door of the garden shed.

'Most of this is rubbish,' she said, 'but if there's anything you'd like to keep, say so now.'

Lola couldn't believe her ears. She was **never** allowed in the shed. It was too messy and dangerous! Also, there were **spiders** in there.

Nick pushed past her.

'I'm having those jam jars. And those broomsticks,' he said. 'And those bike wheels. And −'

'That's enough!' laughed Mum.
'Lola, how about you?'

The shed looked **magical** inside.

Old furniture was jumbled
together, making strange
shapes and shadows on the
walls. Shelves and cupboards
overflowed with tins and jars,
cans and empty pots.

'What's that?' asked Lola. She
pointed to a shape under a sheet.

'Ah,' sighed Mum. 'Take a look.'

'It's mine!' shouted Nick.
'I want it!'

'No, Nick,' said Mum firmly. 'It's Lola's turn to choose something.'

Lola stepped up and pulled the sheet away.

A million specks of dust danced in the sunlight.

And there it was.

A beautiful, somewhat tatty, large wooden box.

'That's not fair,' Nick groaned.

'It's perfect!' said Lola.

CHAPTER TWO

The box looked very, very old. It must have been in the shed for years.

Lola grabbed a cloth from the kitchen and cleaned the dust off the wood.

As she was cleaning, Lola saw some writing inside the lid:

TIMBERFIELDS

Is that a place? Lola wondered. *Perhaps Timberfields is where the box was made.*

The toy box looked much better once it was clean.

Lola and her mum carried the box up to her room.

Her mum went back out to the shed, and Lola picked up Buddy. He was her favourite toy.

Buddy was a learn-to-dress clown. He was covered in buttons and poppers, zippers and buckles. Lola loved him.

'What do you think of my new toy box?' she asked Buddy. 'Does it look like a good home for you and the others?'

Lola often had chats like this with Buddy. He was an excellent listener!

Just then, she heard Nick stomping up the stairs. 'Oi, Lola!' he said loudly. 'I'm coming in to talk about that box.'

Lola sighed. Not **another** Nick attack!

'Go away,' she called back. 'Mum gave the box to **me**.'

'But I want it,' Nick moaned.
'It's not fair! I'll swap you
something. You can have the
bike wheels. Come on, Lola!'

'No,' said Lola. 'The box is mine,
and I'm keeping it.'

Nick was **always** wanting her
stuff. Why couldn't he just leave
her alone?

'I'm counting to five,' Nick
called through the door. 'Then
I'm coming in!'

Sometimes I wish he'd just disappear, Lola thought grumpily.

'One!' called Nick.

Or maybe I could disappear?

'Two!'

I should hide, thought Lola.

'Three!'

She looked at the open toy box. *Of course!*

'Four!'

Lola grabbed Buddy and hopped into the toy box. She shut the lid and crouched inside.

And then **everything** changed.

The box filled with light and began to shake.

What on earth? thought Lola, alarmed.

It was so bright that she had to shut her eyes. She held Buddy tight.

It felt like someone had picked up the toy box and was rattling it around like a money tin! Buddy flew out of her hands and landed in the corner of the box.

Suddenly, the shaking stopped.

Lola waited a second. Then she opened her eyes. Phew!

Leaving Buddy behind, she lifted the lid of the toy box and jumped out.

She felt very cross.

'Nick, what is your **problem**?'
she started to say.

But then she looked around,
and – oh gosh!

Lola had climbed **into** her new
toy box. But she had climbed
out of ...

CHAPTER THREE

She had climbed **out of** a large wooden picnic hamper!

And Lola wasn't in her bedroom anymore. She was on the side of a beautiful hill.

She couldn't believe it.

Things got even **stranger** when Buddy climbed out of the hamper and stood next to her.

Lola stared at her favourite toy. Her mouth opened and closed, but no words came out.

'Bless my buttons, Lola,' Buddy said in a funny voice. 'You look like a goldfish!'

Lola gulped. *Is that …? Is Buddy talking to me?*

Buddy giggled. Then he copied Lola, opening and closing his mouth like a goldfish. He looked very funny.

'But … you're a toy!' said Lola, finally. 'You're …'

'I'm Buddy the Clown,' he said. 'But hey, you know that. You named me!'

Lola nodded. And she shook her head. Then she did both at the same time.

She was smiling. Actually, she was grinning.

'Seeing as you can talk, Buddy,' she said, 'could you tell me where we are? This isn't my bedroom anymore, right?'

Buddy flung his arms out wide.

'Right!' he said. 'Lola, we are in the Kingdom – the most **wonderful** place ever! I'm so happy I could pop my popper.'

Lola grinned even wider.

Pop my popper?

'Do you always talk like that?' she asked.

Buddy looked hurt. 'What's wrong with how I speak?'

'Nothing,' she laughed. 'I love it. I've just never heard it before!'

Buddy was pleased. Then he tried to take a step – but fell over instead!

Lola gasped, and reached down to help poor Buddy.

He was chuckling, though.

'Uh-oh. This might take a while,' Buddy said, standing up again. 'I haven't stood on my own two feet for ages.'

He managed a few **wobbly** steps. Then he tumbled down again. His long legs and laces were all in a tangle!

Lola flopped down next to him. She couldn't stop staring at her favourite toy, who'd somehow come to life.

'Oh Lola, you'll love it here,' said Buddy, grinning back at her.

He took Lola's hand. She helped him stand up on his wonky legs.

Then she got to her feet and looked about, her eyes wide with wonder.

There were beautiful fields all around them. They reminded Lola of the patchwork quilt in her bedroom.

The grass was soft under her feet. She could see odd-shaped trees on the other side of the hill. They looked like … they looked like **toy** trees!

'Tell me all about the Kingdom,' she said, turning back to Buddy.

'Shall we walk as we talk?'
he said happily.

'If you can,' Lola said, smiling.

'Funny girl!' Buddy laughed.
'I'll be fine in no time. Trust
my toggle, I will!'

Then he fell over. And over!

Soon they were strolling and
stumbling down the soft hillside,
carrying the picnic basket
between them.

'The Kingdom is where toys come when they are not being played with by their children,' Buddy explained to Lola.

Lola couldn't believe it. She had **never** thought about what happened to her toys when she wasn't playing with them.

'There are lots of different lands in the Kingdom,' said Buddy. He looked at his wrist, but he wasn't wearing a watch.

'We don't have time for all that now, though,' he added.

'What do you mean?' Lola asked.

Buddy smiled his big goofy clown grin. 'I think we've arrived,' he said, 'just in time for the picnic.'

'The picnic?' repeated Lola.

'Oh yes,' said Buddy cheerfully. 'I have a feeling that today's the day!'

CHAPTER FOUR

They walked through a patch of
toy trees, and then Lola stopped.
She couldn't believe her eyes.
She could see **bears**.

But these weren't real bears.
These were lots and lots of
teddy bears.

There were other toys, too.
Rag dolls and monkeys. Fluffy
cats and soft rabbits. But mostly
teddy bears. They were all sitting
on picnic blankets.

Buddy led Lola to a spare
blanket. They dropped their
picnic basket and sat down.

Buddy was excited. 'By my
buttons, I was right! As soon as
we climbed out of that picnic
hamper, I knew. Today's the day!'

'What day?' asked Lola.

'Today's the day the teddy bears have their picnic!' he said.

Lola laughed. 'They really do that? Amazing!'

Looking around, Lola noticed that she was the only girl among all the toys. She also noticed that none of the toys were eating yet.

Lola's tummy rumbled. What were they waiting for?

Suddenly, everything went silent.

'What's going on?' she whispered.

But Buddy was looking over her shoulder. Lola turned and saw a line of very smart-looking bears coming through the crowd.

This day keeps getting stranger and stranger, she thought.

Then she noticed that one of the bears looked familiar.

Very familiar!

CHAPTER FIVE

'That's Felix!' cried Lola as the bears marched by. 'That's my teddy!'

'Felix is the son of the Great High Bear himself,' Buddy whispered importantly.

Lola was surprised. She had left Felix at her gran's house the last time she'd visited. She wondered if more of her toys were here in the Kingdom.

But what had Buddy said?

That toys only came to the Kingdom when children weren't playing with them?

The bears stopped in the middle of the field. Felix looked around at all the toys.

'Friends!' he called, in a deep bear voice. 'As you know, these are **troubled times** in the Kingdom.'

Felix sounded very serious. Then he said, 'But I bring good news!'

With a flourish, Felix threw open the large picnic box he had been riding on.

Oh good, thought Lola. *Perhaps it's time to eat.*

'I have just returned from Nevercalm!' Felix boomed.

All the toys gasped when they heard this.

Felix lifted up an odd-shaped, plastic wind-up soldier from the basket. 'And we have captured this enemy toy!'

There was another gasp, and then the other toys all started whispering to each other.

Lola stared at the soldier in Felix's paw. It was nodding slowly and its arms moved up and down. It looked lost. She had seen this toy before. But **where**?

'The Plastic Prince has been building an army with soldiers just like this one,' said Felix. 'And he's planning to **attack**!'

Here? Lola was shocked. *In the Kingdom of toys?* But everything seemed so soft and cuddly!

She wondered who the Plastic Prince was, and why he would want to attack.

Buddy seemed to know what Lola was thinking.

'There is a battle going on between the Great High Bear and the Plastic Prince,' he whispered. 'The Great High Bear rules most of the Kingdom. But there is one place, a **scary** place, called Nevercalm.'

Buddy shivered. 'The Plastic Prince rules Nevercalm, and he wants to rule the Kingdom too!'

Lola bit her lip. That sounded serious indeed.

When the crowd became quiet, Felix spoke again.

'Do not worry, friends,' he said, his voice growing louder. 'Today I will show you that the Plastic Prince **cannot** build a strong army. We can prove it.

Watch how easily I can stop this soldier from working!'

In one quick move, Felix pulled the silver key out of the soldier's back. He held it high above his furry ears.

The toys all cheered like **crazy**.

'And that's not all!' Felix yelled.

Lola was worried. **Very** worried. Was Felix going to hurt the toy soldier?

'Without its key,' Felix went on, 'this soldier will soon wind down. And then I'm going to **throw away** the key, and destroy this enemy toy forever!'

Lola jumped to her feet. 'No, Felix!' she shouted at the top of her voice. 'Stop!'

Every single toy in the crowd turned to look at her. Lola felt the blood rushing to her cheeks.

Then a tiny voice beside her said, 'Oh, Lola, I hope you know what you're doing. By my **zipper**, I do!'

CHAPTER SIX

Felix walked towards Lola.

Buddy shuffled in closer.

'Well, well, well,' said Felix

darkly. 'If it isn't my dear Lola.

How very nice to see you.'

Lola wasn't sure he actually meant that.

'What are you doing in the Kingdom?' Felix asked. 'It has been a long, long time since we've had a real girl here.'

Then Buddy spoke up.

'Oh, she's just here with me, Felix,' he said, his voice trembling. 'For fun. For a picnic. And we were just leaving, actually.'

'Hello, Buddy,' said Felix quietly.
'It's been a long time since we've
seen you here, too.'

He rubbed his furry chin. He
looked at Lola and then Buddy.

'Lola,' he said, 'this soldier
works for the Plastic Prince, our
enemy. But you don't think we
should destroy it. Why is that?'

The soldier was still quietly
nodding its head, up and down,
up and down.

The toy was getting slower, and making a quiet humming noise.

Lola took a good look at Felix. He was a very fine bear. He had neat, orange fur and a stern look on his face.

Lola felt a bit nervous. But she also felt sure that Felix shouldn't hurt the poor soldier. She took a deep breath.

'I don't think we should be **cruel**,' Lola said. 'To anything or anyone.'

Felix nodded and was silent
for a long time.

Finally, in a very **strange** voice,
he said, 'OK. I won't throw the
key away. You can keep it. On
one condition.'

A funny feeling crept into Lola's
tummy. But it wasn't a **good**
funny feeling.

Felix drew himself up to his full
height. 'The condition is that
you first pass a test.'

Buddy sprang forward. 'Blast my buckle!' he cried. 'You can't be serious, Felix.'

'I am the son of the Great High Bear,' said Felix, angrily. 'Lola has challenged my orders. How do we know we can trust her?'

A whisper ran through the crowd. It sounded like the toys were all saying, 'Buttons! Buttons! Buttons!'

'Indeed, she will do the button test!' Felix said loudly. 'And if she fails, I will destroy this enemy toy – and Lola will **never** be allowed back in the Kingdom!'

Then he turned back to Lola. 'Do you accept?'

Lola gulped. She knew this test was **very** important.

She had loved coming to the Kingdom. It was amazing seeing all these toys come alive.

She'd never had a **real**
adventure like this before.
And she'd be sad if she
couldn't come back.

But then Lola looked over
at the poor toy soldier. *What
will happen to him if I say no?*

'I accept,' she said firmly.

A thrill ran through her body
as the crowd of toys began
cheering.

CHAPTER SEVEN

'Very well,' Felix said seriously.
'Let's get ready.'

Felix took a golden button from
one pocket and a silver button
from the other. Then he turned
to Buddy and held out a paw.

Buddy seemed to know what to do. He handed Felix one of his own buttons. It was a very plain, old wooden button.

Felix lined up the buttons on the picnic hamper. Then he handed Lola a rolled up piece of paper. It was tied with a ribbon.

'If you pass this test, we will know that you can be trusted,' Felix told her.

All the toys were **silent**.

Lola could feel the eyes of every bear and rag doll and cat and monkey and rabbit – on **her**.

She pulled the ribbon and unrolled the paper. Her hands were shaking.

Then she began to read aloud, and her voice was shaking too:

THE BUTTON TEST

You must choose **one** button.

Gold will bring you **riches**,
your dreams of **wealth** come true.
And all the joy that **money** brings
will surely come to you.

Silver brings you **bravery**
and **skills** to win the fight.
You'll stand up tall and **fearless,**
with all your **strength** and might.

Wooden buttons seldom break,
they just go **on and on.**
So they will surely **serve** you well,
when other things have **gone.**

CHAPTER EIGHT

When Lola had finished reading, she looked at the three buttons on top of the picnic hamper. Gold, silver and wood.

Gold. The gold button looked so beautiful and shiny in the sunlight.

Lola liked the idea of having lots of money. There were loads of things she'd love to buy. New pens. New toys. A new **bike**.

I could have anything I want, thought Lola.

Silver. The silver button looked smart, like it was from a uniform. Lola liked the idea of being braver and stronger.

It might help me stand up to Nick, she thought.

Lastly, **wood**. Next to the gold and silver buttons, Buddy's wooden one looked a bit tatty. It wasn't fancy. But it would last forever. And it came from her favourite toy in the world.

Lola read the poem again.

Then she took a deep breath, grabbed a button, and held it up for all to see.

All the toys stared.

Then there was the very strange
sound of hundreds of soft paws
and fabric hands clapping.

'Well done, Lola,' said Felix.
His whole face had changed.
He was smiling and nodding.
'Well done!'

Lola felt a grin spread across her
face. 'It was easy in the end,' she
said, looking at the wooden
button in her hand. 'I don't
need riches and shiny new stuff.

And I can be brave and strong all by myself. But this button is special to me, because it came from my friend Buddy.'

The crowd of toys whooped and clapped.

'Hooray!' they cheered. 'Hooray for Lola!'

Lola laughed and looked around for Buddy. He was busy doing some very unsteady cartwheels.

'I am glad you chose well,' Felix told her. He was still smiling ear to ear.

Then he raised his voice and yelled, 'Lola will be **forever welcome** in the Kingdom!'

CHAPTER NINE

While all the other toys were still eating, Lola and Felix sat back against the big picnic basket. Buddy was swinging from the tree above them.

The wind-up soldier had stopped moving now.

But Lola wasn't worried about it. She had the key.

Felix was acting like a very different bear now. He wasn't stern and stuffy anymore. Lola was happy to have her old teddy back.

Felix turned to Lola. 'I'm sorry I was so bossy before,' he said softly. 'But I was cross. You used to play with me all the time. And then one day you just **forgot** about me.'

Lola looked at her feet. She felt very guilty. 'I know,' she said. 'I'm sorry, Felix. Kids forget their toys all the time. Even the ones they love. We're silly that way.'

Felix sighed. 'It's OK,' he said. 'I'm not the first toy to be left behind somewhere. I'm glad I got to see you again. And at least I've been able to spend time with my father here in the Kingdom.'

Lola gave Felix a big bear hug. Then she stretched out on the soft grass as Felix and Buddy chatted about the Plastic Prince and Nevercalm.

After that, they moved on to other toys they knew, from towns like Cuddleton, Patchemup and Timberfields.

Timberfields? thought Lola with a start. *Where have I heard that name before?*

Buddy was surprised that so much had changed in the Kingdom. His last visit had been a long time ago.

'But I bet my buttons we'll beat that Plastic Prince,' Buddy kept saying.

Lola didn't understand why **anyone** would want to start a war against the Great High Bear and the Kingdom. Why was the Plastic Prince so mean?

She wanted to know more, but it was getting late.

Lola stood up and brushed the grass off her legs. 'Buddy, how do we get home? Mum will be wondering where I am.'

'The same way we came,' he replied, opening the lid of their picnic hamper.

Lola looked at Felix. 'Do you want to come home too?'

Felix shook his head. 'I am needed here,' he said. 'But you must return to the Kingdom soon. We could do with a real girl like you. You're very kind.'

Lola nodded. She knew she and Buddy would return for sure.

Then she carefully lifted the toy soldier into the picnic hamper. She remembered now where she had seen it before.

Felix looked worried that she was taking the soldier, but Lola just smiled. 'It's OK,' she said. 'I know what I'm doing.'

After some more big bear hugs, Lola and Buddy hopped back into the picnic hamper.

Well, they climbed **into** the hamper. But Lola climbed **out of** ...

CHAPTER TEN

Lola climbed **out of** her toy box. She was safe and sound, back in her bedroom.

And Nick was still banging on the door. 'If I get to five, there's going to be trouble!' he shouted.

Lola opened her bedroom door.

'Sorry, Nick,' she said. 'I didn't hear you.'

'That's impossible,' he hissed. 'I was **shouting**, Lola.'

'Well, please don't,' said Lola, folding her arms. 'It's not nice to shout. It's not **kind**.'

Nick's mouth dropped open. But Lola stood there, looking calmly at her brother.

Nick wasn't used to this. Lola could see the **surprise** in his eyes.

'You're not having the toy box, Nick,' she said quietly.

'Oh, yeah?' he said, but she could tell he was confused.

Lola had a funny feeling in her tummy. It was almost the same feeling she'd had before she stood up to Felix at the picnic.

And that gave her an idea.

'It's a toy box, Nick,' she said firmly. 'For my toys. And it belongs to me.'

'Rubbish,' said Nick, but he didn't look at all sure now.

Then Lola held out the odd little plastic soldier that she'd brought back from the Kingdom. 'But this toy,' she said, 'belongs to you.'

Nick's eyes lit up. 'Wow! I've been looking for that for ages.'

He grabbed the soldier out of her hand and looked at it eagerly.

Lola grinned. 'You might need this too,' she said, handing him the little silver key.

Nick snatched it and marched off. He didn't seem at all interested in the toy box anymore.

Lola wasn't sure what had just happened, but it felt good.

She sat on her bed and took a long, hard look at the toy box.

Was that all a dream? wondered Lola. *Was it all in my imagination?*

Lola lifted Buddy up. One of his buttons was missing.

She reached into her pocket, and there it was.

The wooden button.

At that moment, Lola knew for
sure. It was **all** real.

Just then, she heard Mum calling
from downstairs. 'Lola, how's
that old toy box?' she asked.
'Is it any good?'

Lola laughed. She held Buddy
tight and jumped back into the
toy box.

Just before she closed the lid,
she called back, 'Oh, Mum!
It's magic!'

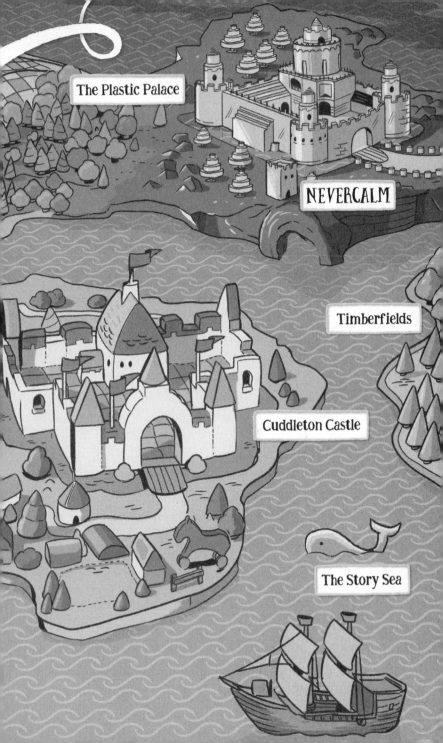

The Plastic Palace

NEVERCALM

Timberfields

Cuddleton Castle

The Story Sea

ABOUT THE
AUTHOR & ILLUSTRATOR

Danny Parker is a writer and drama teacher who lives in Perth with his family. His previous books include *Tree* and *Parachute*. Danny is a keen juggler, singer and performer – just like Buddy!

Guy Shield is an illustrator who lives in Melbourne and is obsessed with drawing. When he was a kid, Guy loved building palaces and cities with his toys, just like Lola – and Nick!

Lola's TOY BOX

When Lola is given an old toy box, she discovers it's a magical passageway ... to a world where toys come to life!

Join Lola and Buddy on all their adventures into the toy box Kingdom and beyond!

You can follow Lola and Buddy into the Kingdom at
www.lolastoybox.com.au

Available in all good bookshops & libraries.